MONSTER ROOMS HANDBOOK

To claim your surprise freebie, go to the sign-in page of

MOSHIMONSTERS.COM

and enter the ninth word on the fifteenth line of the fifty-sixth page of this book! Your free virtual gift will appear in your Treasure Chest!

GROSSET & DUNLAP
Published by the Penguin Group
Penguin Group (USA) Inc., 375 Hudson Street, New York, New York 10014, USA
Penguin Group (Canada), 90 Eglinton Avenue East, Suite 700,
Toronto, Ontario M4P 2Y3, Canada
(a division of Pearson Penguin Canada Inc.)
Penguin Books Ltd, 80 Strand, London WC2R 0RL, England
Penguin Ireland, 25 St Stephen's Green, Dublin 2, Ireland
(a division of Penguin Books Ltd)
Penguin Group (Australia), 707 Collins Street, Melbourne, Victoria 3008, Australia
(a division of Pearson Australia Group Pty Ltd)
Penguin Books India Pvt Ltd, 11 Community Centre,
Panchsheel Park, New Delhi—110 017, India
Penguin Group (NZ), 67 Apollo Drive, Rosedale, Auckland 0632, New Zealand
(a division of Pearson New Zealand Ltd)
Penguin Books (South Africa), Rosebank Office Park, 181 Jan Smuts Avenue,
Parktown North 2193, South Africa
Penguin China, B7 Jiaming Center, 27 East Third Ring Road North,
Chaoyang District, Beijing 100020, China

Penguin Books Ltd, Registered Offices: 80 Strand, London WC2R 0RL, England

The publisher does not have any control over and does not assume any responsibility for author or third-party websites or their content.

First printed in Great Britain in 2011 by Ladybird Books Ltd. First published in the United States in 2013 by Grosset & Dunlap, a division of Penguin Young Readers Group, 345 Hudson Street, New York, New York 10014. GROSSET & DUNLAP is a trademark of Penguin Group (USA) Inc. Manufactured in China.

ISBN 978-0-448-46748-1   10 9 8 7 6 5 4 3 2 1

ALWAYS LEARNING   PEARSON

MONSTAR ROOMS HANDBOOK

Grosset & Dunlap
An Imprint of Penguin Group (USA) Inc.

CONTENTS

TYRA FANGS—HOME-FASHION EXPERT!

When I'm not at my job as a judge at the Underground Disco or getting much-needed retail therapy from the Marketplace, I'm probably on one of my famous home-fashion tours across Monstro City. That's right, I LOVE to snoop around everybody's homes and see what trends are hot right now.

I've picked up a LOT of inspiring ideas while poking around the houses of Monstro City, so I thought I would share them with the world in this handy home handbook. Check out my hip tips on how to create a MonSTAR room of your very own.

CATCH MY EYE

Monsters often ask me what I'm looking for on my home-fashion tours. Here are a few hints to make your room stand out!

1. Keep it colorful! Fruity brights, sparkling jewel shades, and loud neons really make a room rock!

2. Make it comfortable! Like any monster, I can see the appeal of a nice damp cave, but, hey, this lady likes a bit of luxury!

3. Sometimes, less is more! There's so much great stuff in the stores of Monstro City, it can be tempting to buy, buy, buy! I'm all for shopping, but make sure you have room to display it all—there's no point in having a Cuddly Ninja if it's buried under a pile of Bowler Balls!

4. Be original! I've seen a lot of monster rooms on my travels, so dare to be different and put your own mark on your room by doing something new!

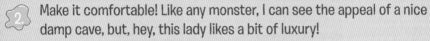

BLINGING YOUR BASE!

Okay, so you've adopted a monster and you have your very own room to keep it in, but it's looking a bit plain. What you need to do is decorate! But wait, before we head down to the stores, here's how you get started.

THE CHEST

Whenever you buy items (except clothes) from the stores in Monstro City, they'll go into your Treasure Chest. Click on the chest to open it and take a look inside. It might be empty now, but when you want to take something out of it, you can drag and drop the item into your room.

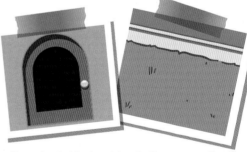

If you're taking out basic items—walls, floors, doors, or windows—just drop them anywher in the room and the room will change. The ol part of the room will end up in your chest, to be used later if you want to.

If you're putting furniture or any other item into the room, decide where you want to put it and drop it in. You can move it around as much as you like, but only while the chest is open. Smaller items can be put on shelves or tables and some items can be hung from the walls or ceiling.

Food items from the Gross-ery store have to be dropped right onto your monster to feed them and can't be left around the room. If your monster isn't hungry, you can keep the food in your chest until next time. Make sure you close your chest to continue playing the game.

Tyra's Hip Tip

Everyone loves presents, and your monster is no exception! Each item you buy for your monster gives it happy points which improve your monster's mood. The cooler the item, the happier it's going to make your monster.
Go for the more expensive items—it pays off in happy points. Nobody wants a grumpy monster! And for a superquick cheat, just give your monster a tickle for extra happy points!

LET'S GO SHOPPING!

Monsters love to shop till they drop, and Monstro City is the perfect place for retail therapy. There are lots of stores to choose from, with new ones popping up all the time. Here are a few of my favorite places to shop . . .

MAIN STREET

Yukea—If you're into great design and fair prices, then Yukea is your place for room basics. These colorful classics make a great backdrop for all the cool stuff you'll buy around town. The Shark Cabinet is a *fin*-tastic way to display your trophies, and while the Backwards Puzzle Clock won't make you go back in time, it will help you at the Puzzle Palace.

Gross-ery—Any monster knows that shopping is a hungry business, so don't forget to stop off at the Gross-ery and stock up on snacks and treats! You'll have to feed your monster to keep its health up. I highly recommend a starter of Garlic Marshmallow, followed by a Crab 'n' Jelly Sandwich, all washed down with Bug Juice. Monsters LOVE dessert, so you might want to grab some Sludge Fudge, too.

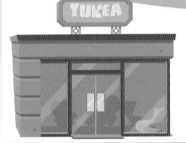

Bizarre Bazaar—Bushy Fandango keeps the Bizarre Bazaar fully stocked with some seriously strange stuff. Start your collections of Cuddly Humans and Bowler Balls here. I recommend the Yellow Jelly Floor to put a spring in your monster's step, or the collectible Dino the Dino bones for that Jurassic-lark feel. Roary Scrawl loves the Purple Eyes Wallpaper, since it reminds him of his mommy. Aah.

Seed Cart—Pick up some seeds while you're out to get your garden going! Find out what they're for on page 56!

Horrods—Discerning Moshi Members with true monster-chic should browse at Horrods. Mizz Snoots stocks all kinds of daring décor, including the incredibly rare statue of *The Stinker* and the even rarer Platinum Pants of Power—snap these up if you see them. Who knows when they'll be on sale again?

DIY Shop—Dewy has some of the funkiest and freakiest furniture in town, as well as a huge range of basics to get your chosen theme off to a great start. I love to snuggle up on my Raarghly Bear Rug—this cuddly snoozing squished bear looks awesome and comes with tons of happiness points to keep your monster smiling.

Games Starcade—You'll need to be a member with mega Rox to shop here, but it's well worth saving up for one of these awesome arcade games. Now you don't even need to leave home to play, and even better, you can get your friends to play, too! Find out more on page 54.

Marketplace—Ah, fashion! Whether it's monster-style or interior design, I love it! The Marketplace is bursting with clothes and accessories for every kind of monster. If you've got an amazing theme going on in your room, why not extend it to your monster's clothes, too? Choose from a wide variety of mustaches, bow ties, hats, jewelery, and more!

LET'S GO SHOPPING!

Dodgy Dealz—Dodgy Dealz is not quite a store, but definitely worth a look if you're low on Rox. Sly Chance sloped into Monstro City from the Shifty Shack Sandbar and set up business at the far end of Sludge Street. If you have spare stuff and want to take your chances on making some quick Rox, Dodgy Dealz is the place to bring your unwanted items. Sly doesn't want your old clothes or seeds though, so you can't trade those.

As soon as you walk through the door, Sly will take a look at what you've got to deal with. Place the item you want to trade in his chest and he'll make you an offer. You can either take his deal or gamble! There's no trick to the gambling. It's all in the luck of the draw, so you could get back the Rox you spent on the item, or lose them all . . . They don't call it Dodgy Dealz for nothing, you know!

MOSHI MEMBERS SHOPS AT THE PORT

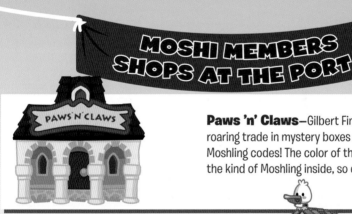

Paws 'n' Claws—Gilbert Finnster does a roaring trade in mystery boxes that contain secret Moshling codes! The color of the box is a clue to the kind of Moshling inside, so choose carefully!

Babs' Boutique—Babs' stocks all kinds of cool collectibles, like WallScrawl letters, Scare Bears, and Beanie Blobs, as well as some great theme-room items. Find out more about collecting on page 46!

The Cloudy Cloth Clipper—Cap'n Buck E. Barnacle's pirate ship holds a boatload of booty! Buck is often off on his travels, but Moshi Members should keep an eye out for his random returns to the port. Roary Scrawl reports his comings and goings in the *Daily Growl*. When his ship is there, Buck's shop has all kinds of treasures, depending on where he's been, from Futuristic Falls to Cookhouse Quay and Bubblebath Bay. Each haul has a different theme, so collect it all while you get the chance, before he sails away again. Score your monster some serious happy points with these items:

BUBBLE BATH
Clean up your monster's act and put a smile on its face with this bubblicious bath!
80 Rox
104 happy points

TURBO TOASTER
To make the perfect Jelly Baked Beans on toast!
108 Rox
110 happy points

ROBOT BUTLER
When you get your butler home, give him a little click to wake him up and see what happens . . .
115 Rox
250 happy points

DOODLE ISLAND DOOR
The wax from the crayons will stop your door from creaking!
167 Rox
173 happy points

THE BASICS

There are four things no monster's room should be without—a floor, walls, a door, and some windows! Your brand-new room has all these things, but look how dull they are! Getting rid of these and getting some shiny new ones is the best way to get started with the decorating . . .

DOORS

Pretty crucial for getting in and out of rooms, unless you're a Luvli or a Diavlo and are happy floating in and out of the window. If you're on the lower levels, these elegant entrances could work for you:

PINK DOOR
Ah, one for pretty, girly monsters!
23 Rox

SURFBOARD DOOR
For surfer dudes and dudettes!
53 Rox

TRADITIONAL WHITE DOOR
The most doorlike door there is. No confusion.
82 Rox

WALLS

Handy for holding up the roof, the walls are also the main canvas for your monster's room! Last time I checked, Monstro City had over sixty types of wallpaper on sale, and the Wobbly Wallpaper Workers are always coming up with new designs! Here are some of my favorites to look out for:

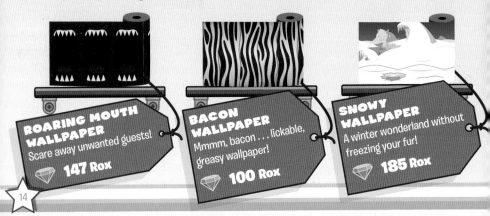

ROARING MOUTH WALLPAPER
Scare away unwanted guests!
147 Rox

BACON WALLPAPER
Mmmm, bacon . . . lickable, greasy wallpaper!
100 Rox

SNOWY WALLPAPER
A winter wonderland without freezing your fur!
185 Rox

FLOORS

Better than falling into an enormous hole, floors are also fairly important. But this practical room feature doesn't have to be boring—oh, no. Why not try one of these funky floorings?

CLOUD FLOOR
You'll always be on cloud nine with this fluffy floor!
💎 **78 Rox**

STAGE ROOM FLOOR
To bring out the star in your monster!
💎 **91 Rox**

BUBBLE FLOOR
For the cleanest monster toes in town!
💎 **122 Rox**

WINDOWS

Great for seeing out of, even better for peeking in and checking out other monsters' rooms! Here are some wild windows to look out for:

DOODLE ISLAND WINDOW
With curtains already drawn!
💎 **89 Rox**

HEART WINDOW
For monsters in love.
💎 **162 Rox**

SEAWEED WINDOW
Mmm, soggy!
💎 **49 Rox**

Tyra's Hip Tip

There are lots of theme items to be found in the stores of Monstro City, so whether you want your room to look like a moonscape, a circus, a stage, or even a garage, there's something out there for you! I've picked out some of my favorite themes on pages 20-41, but there are lots more out there. Some items and themes are only available to buy once you reach a certain level, so, as Roary says, always keep your eyes at hand when out shopping!

FURNITURE

Now that you have the basics in place, it's time to get your monster some creature comforts! I've done my research and picked out some great pieces for you to take a look at, but there are plenty more to choose from if these aren't to your taste! New stuff arrives in the stores all the time, so keep checking back!

CHAIRS
Pull up a seat and get comfy!

BREAKFAST BAYOU SAUSAGE SOFA
Sausage-roll pillows not included.
90 Rox

CHAIR OF THE FUTURE
Apparently, everything is more pointy in the future.
40 Rox

BARF-ALONA CHAIR
Superstylish and only slightly sticky!
54 Rox

TABLES
A great way to display your favorite purchases.

FOOT TABLE
Now made with real feet!
61 Rox

BOULDER TABLE
Rock plus rock equals table. Sort of.
45 Rox

ICE BLOCK TABLE
Just don't put anything hot on it.
98 Rox

SHELVES

Perfect for showing off trophies and collectibles.

BAMBOO CABINET
ShiShi thinks it's rather tasty . . .
💎 **59 Rox**

WROUGHT IRON CABINET
For only the fanciest monsters.
💎 **119 Rox**

FLUTTERBY CABINET
For your monster's prized possessions.
💎 **88 Rox**

FREAKY FEATURES

There are tons of great ways to add the finishing touches to your room— here are just a few of my favorites!

HAPPY SMILEY OVEN
For happy smiley food!
💎 **91 Rox**

IRON FURNACE
For warming your monster's toes.
💎 **173 Rox**

FRIED EGG RUG
Prefried for your convenience.
💎 **114 Rox**

STUFF, GLORIOUS STUFF!

In my humble opinion, a monster's home isn't complete without stuff. Tons of it. Trophies, knickknacks, posters, and collectibles—whatever keeps your monster happy. Pile it in . . . These items are the best, so get your paws on them if you see them in the stores!

THE COOLEST OF THE COOL

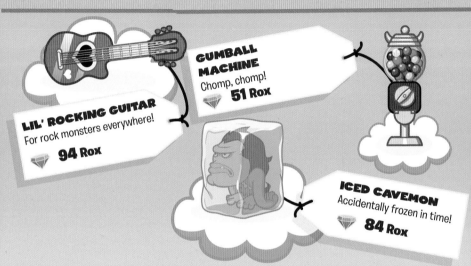

GUMBALL MACHINE
Chomp, chomp!
💎 **51 Rox**

LIL' ROCKING GUITAR
For rock monsters everywhere!
💎 **94 Rox**

ICED CAVEMON
Accidentally frozen in time!
💎 **84 Rox**

THE STRANGEST OF THE STRANGE

EVIL SOCK PUPPET
Muahahaha!
💎 **99 Rox**

SHARK BOWL
More interesting than your usual fishbowl . . .
💎 **103 Rox**

BAT MOBILE
(Robin not included.)
💎 **96 Rox**

THE CUTEST OF THE CUTE

MY LITTLE MUTANT
A speedy little pony with six legs!

💎 **91 Rox**

PET SEA HORSE
Fish, schmish! All the modern monsters have sea horses!

💎 **153 Rox**

CATACACTUS
Me-ow! It's a spiky one!

💎 **117 Rox**

CUDDLY MOSHLINGS!

💎 **39-85 Rox**

THE RAREST OF THE RARE

JACK-IN-THE-BOX
Just turn the handle and . . . AAARGH!

💎 **111 Rox**

EGYPTIAN CAT STATUE
This will look great in your tomb, er . . . room!

💎 **190 Rox**

PRINCESS POPPET MUSIC BOX
Wind her up and watch her go!

💎 **128 Rox**

Tyra's Hip Tip

When you get your stuff home and your new knickknacks have taken pride of place in your room, give them a little click. Sometimes nothing happens, but some objects move or make noises, so you never quite know what you're getting! Watch out, though; not all of them are friendly . . .

SIMPLY SPACE

Ever feel like your sense of style is light-years ahead of the rest? Want to skyrocket your room's rating and run Saturn rings around your friends?

SIMPLY SPACE ROOM BASICS

WALLS

Before you head up into space, you'll need the ultimate in rocket-travel essentials. Try either the Navy Blue or Black as Night Wallpapers. Then head over to Babs' Boutique to buy the WallScrawl Shooting Star and WallScrawl Moon and bring that sparkly night sky right inside.

BLACK AS NIGHT WALLPAPER Any color as long as it's black.
💎 **77 Rox**

WALLSCRAWL SHOOTING STAR
💎 **72 Rox**

WALLSCRAWL MOON Made from real moon flakes.
💎 **45 Rox**

FLOORS, DOORS, AND WINDOWS

A Metal Grate Floor will work particularly well in your space room. *Clink! Clink! Clink!* And fully reinforce against alien attacks with the metal windows. For superspacey options try the Vortex Door, the Door to Another World, or the Trip to the Moon Window!

METAL GRATE FLOOR Cold on monster toes!
💎 **64 Rox**

VORTEX DOOR It's almost not quite there.
💎 **37 Rox**

TRIP TO THE MOON WINDOW
💎 **77 Rox**

SIMPLY SPACE FITTINGS AND FURNISHINGS

No space room is complete without these galactic goodies!

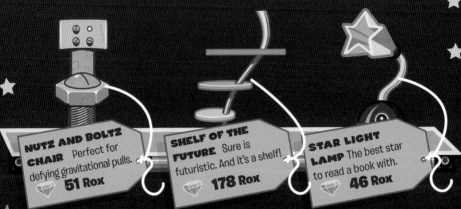

NUTZ AND BOLTZ CHAIR Perfect for defying gravitational pulls.
💎 **51 Rox**

SHELF OF THE FUTURE Sure is futuristic. And it's a shelf!
💎 **178 Rox**

STAR LIGHT LAMP The best star to read a book with.
💎 **46 Rox**

SIMPLY SPACE FINISHING TOUCHES

Finish off your space look with some of these cosmic added extras.

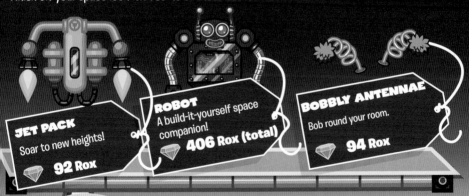

JET PACK Soar to new heights!
💎 **92 Rox**

ROBOT A build-it-yourself space companion!
💎 **406 Rox (total)**

BOBBLY ANTENNAE Bob round your room.
💎 **94 Rox**

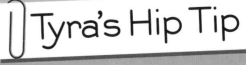

Tyra's Hip Tip

Remember not to clutter your room with too much stuff. You'll need some space to chill out under the stars!

PRINCESS CASTLE

If, like most princesses, you simply have to shop in Horrods, love dressing in fancy clothes, and eat nothing but Grande Gateaux, then a perfect princess-castle room is your essential accessory. Here's how to create an extravagant room fit for a princess. (With the help of your servants, of course!)

CASTLE MUST-HAVES

Walls

Try the Castle Wallpaper to show off the fact that you are living in an absolutely enormous and incredibly expensive castle. Or dabble in a little of the exquisite, with the Fleur de Lys Wallpaper. Add a generous touch of princess sparkle throughout, with some WallScrawl Sparkles. And remember—presentation is key.

FLEUR DE LYS WALLPAPER

💎 **47 Rox**

Windows

Castles might look fabulously grand from the outside, but they can sometimes be a little grimy inside. Purchase the Castle Windows and let lots of luscious light in. You could also find some Curtain Windows—ah, curtains, what a luxury!

CASTLE WINDOWS

💎 **72 Rox**

Floors

Try out the Quilted Floor—couldn't you just fall asleep on this? You wouldn't, of course, as princesses should only sleep on beautiful four-poster beds, thrones, and chaise lounges. But walking on the quilted floor will help take care of your precious little princess feet.

QUILTED FLOOR

💎 **45 Rox**

Fancy Frilly Furnishings

A princess castle is all about the lavish finishes and decorative delights! Try the exquisite matching Wrought Iron Table and Cabinet. Or the Vanity Table—it may be 179 Rox, but you're worth it, so buy it! Or how about the Chaise Lounge? Or the Crystal Chandelier—need we explain why? And what castle is furnished without a Fancy Table? Come on, you know you want it!

CHAISE LOUNGE
Perfect for lounging during princess duties!
💎 **124 Rox**

VANITY TABLE
For when you just want to stare at yourself in the mirror . . .
💎 **179 Rox**

WROUGHT IRON CABINET
For only the fanciest monsters.
💎 **119 Rox**

Perfecting That Castle Look

Go out and buy your very own princess Magic Mirror—look deep into it and see if you can unlock its mystical powers. Then, express your good taste by buying a Monsta Lisa Painting. Is she smiling? Is she frowning? Is she a monster? And don't forget the Shakesfear Bust—the most famous writer in Monstro City, author of *Groaneo and Spewliet*.

MAGIC MIRROR
💎 **23 Rox**

MONSTA LISA PAINTING
💎 **88 Rox**

SHAKESFEAR BUST
💎 **351 Rox**

Tyra's Hip Tip

Always dress to impress and buy a Frilly White Dress and some Fairy Wings or a flowing green Royal Gown. Complete the royal look by purchasing a Princess Headdress for 96 Rox.

THE FOREST

For those of you who love the great outdoors and are looking to create your very own woodland wonderland, there are fields full of fantastic forest furnishings for you to buy in Monstro City. With these simple suggestions, you can build the perfect forest habitat fit for you, your Moshlings, and lots of other wildlife.

The Basic Outdoors Be at one with nature by slapping up some of the Forest Wallpaper. Buy the Forest Floor, too, and tickle your monster's toes with the lovely grass floor. Complete that outside/inside look by buying the Forest Windows. Then, climb through your very own Forest Door to Monstro City and beyond.

FOREST WALLPAPER
💎 **215 Rox**

FOREST DOOR
💎 **114 Rox**

PINE WINDOW
💎 **21 Rox**

LEAVES WINDOW
💎 **61 Rox**

GRASSY WINDOW
💎 **15 Rox**

Windows for All Seasons Buy a nice Pine Window for your wall—it has its own built-in fresh scent of pine! Alternatively, a lovely Leaves Window will bring that autumn feel to your windows. When it comes to summertime, go for the Grassy Window— haven't you always wished you could have a window covered in grass?

MEADOW GREEN WALLPAPER
💎 **20** Rox

DARK GREEN WALLPAPER
💎 **21** Rox

BUTTERFLIES WALLPAPER
💎 **81** Rox

Weelly Wild Wallpaper Try putting up the Meadow Green wallpaper and ruuuuun freeeeeeeee! Or if you just have a thing for green, you can't get any greener than the Dark Green Wallpaper. Alternatively, go all fluttery and buttery with the Butterflies Wallpaper, which will set you back a mere 81 Rox.

BAMBOO CABINET
💎 **59** Rox

BAMBOO TABLE
💎 **21** Rox

BIRD'S NEST
💎 **99** Rox

Forest Furnishings Get some bamboo furniture such as the Bamboo Cabinet, which is sturdily constructed but prone to sneezing panda attacks. Then add a Bird's Nest to your wall—*Twit twoo! Twit twoo!* That's Birdish for "cool nest," donchaknow?!

Flowery Finishes Buy a Smiley Flower or two to finish the forest—how can you help but smile with such happy flowers?

SMILEY FLOWERS
💎 **98** Rox

Tyra's Hip Tip

Moshlings love being outside, so get as many as you can that love trees! If you're a Moshi Member, you can even buy the Birdies Bird House for 32 Rox at Paws 'n' Claws, which is sure to make your Birdies chirp with delight.

DISCO DIGS

It's time to turn your room into the ultimate disco party pad, where everyone will want to dance the night away, then chill with all the cool cats. Follow the rehearsal dance tips below to get your room looking good before you have a big dance-off!

DISCO LIGHTS
💎 **188 Rox**

LAVA LAMP
💎 **55 Rox**

Dance Tip 1—Get into the Mood and Heat It Up . . . A Lava Lamp will help with the chilled mood, but make sure you also buy the Disco Lights, so you're sure to rock the house. D-d-d-dance eveeerrrrybooooodyyy!

Dance Tip 2—Keep It Smooth . . .
Use lots of soft furnishings and deck out your pad with a Furry Luv Chair—a comfy, fuzzy chair—far out!

FURRY LUV CHAIR
💎 **101 Rox**

Dance Tip 3—Get into the Groove . . .
Disco Ball—hang it from your ceiling, and your monster will get its funk on with style!

DISCO BALL
💎 **118 Rox**

Dance Tip 4—Make It as Funky as Can Be . . . Purchase a F-f-funky Window and Door to f-f-funk up your room and bend space and time, so you can dance from the *f* to the *o* to the *r* to the *e* to the *v* to the *e* to the *r*—FOREVER!

F-F-FUNKY DOOR
💎 **58 Rox**

Dance Tip 5 — Then Heat It Up Some More . . . Try some retro smokin'-hot Bacon Wallpaper and feel the heat as you dance!

BACON WALLPAPER
100 Rox

FURRY FLOOR
94 Rox

Dance Tip 6—Now You're Ready to Take It to the Dance Floor . . . If chilling is your thing, go for a soft-under-the-foot Furry Floo—now made with artificial fur. But for those of you who are all about the dancing, get yourself the Checkered Floor, perfect for breakdancing!

Disco Dress No dynamite disco-diva outfit is complete without some Flamin' Shades. Get them hot off the shelves, now! Or try the Sweatband—a must-have if dancing is your thang—or Platforms: Stand up tall and say, "I am nearly as big as a Furi!"

FLAMIN' SHADES
51 Rox

Extra Essentials You should be ready by now, so buy the Big Bad Boom Box in Blueberry Blue or Pomegranate Pink and dance the night away! If you need refreshment just grab yourself a Fango Mandango—a dancing fruit that will get you moving again!

BLUEBERRY BLUE BOOM BOX
57 Rox

POMEGRANATE PINK BOOM BOX
65 Rox

CHECK YOU LATER, CATS-BE COOL.

HAUNTED HOUSE

Now you can enjoy Halloween year-round with your very own spooky Haunted House room. Create a cool yet creepy hangout where you can howl at the moon as you wish, chomp on Crispy Batwings, RIP (rest in peace) whenever you want, and scare anyone who dares to visit your room . . . Boo! Ha-ha-ha! Adopt a total Haunted House style and follow the scary footsteps below to realize the room of your nightmares!

Wonderful Wallpaper

Try the Purple Eyes Wallpaper for your walls—it's *eye*-mazing. You can then upgrade at a later date to the More Purple Eyes Wallpaper—eyes and eyes and nothing but eyes. Or the Bats Wallpaper would also work very, very well!

PURPLE EYES WALLPAPER
💎 85 Rox

BATS WALLPAPER
💎 87 Rox

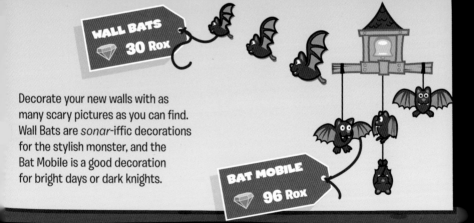

WALL BATS
💎 30 Rox

Decorate your new walls with as many scary pictures as you can find. Wall Bats are *sonar*-iffic decorations for the stylish monster, and the Bat Mobile is a good decoration for bright days or dark knights.

BAT MOBILE
💎 96 Rox

The Perfect Place to Sit

Get yourself a Scare Chair—I don't know about you, but I'm not sure I'd sit on it. Then again, it's a great place to sit down and chomp on a bowl of Pumpkin Chowder—best served on Halloween.

SCARE CHAIR
💎 165 Rox

SPIDER CHANDELIER
💎 71 Rox

Frightening Lighting

Spider Chandelier—hang out with the spider that simply hangs from your ceiling.

Eerie Extras

No haunted habitat is complete without Monsieur Macabre's Mansion, so definitely buy one, but whatever you do, don't unleash the ghouls! And tuck into some Roarberry Cheesecake—the cake that bites back!

ROARBERRY CHEESECAKE
💎 45 Rox

SPIDER DARTBOARD
💎 46 Rox

Evil Entertainment

Spider Dartboard—webbed fun for all the family (not suitable for flies under twelve).

Tyra's Hip Tip

Blend into your new dark and gloomy room by being a Wicked Witch for the day. Buy the Witch Broom, Dress, Hat, and Enchanted Hair that is always as black as the blackest night. Then, top off your costume with a gruesomely green Wicked Witch Nose. Alternatively, you could pick up the Vampy's Cloak—mwuhaha! Vampy's Fangs are also a must with this—a vampy isn't a vampy without zis pair of vicious-looking fangs.

UNDER THE SEA

Splash into an underwater world and ride the waves of sea-room chic with a dangers-of-the-deep dive or super surfing shack. Choose a relaxed beach hangout or immerse yourself deep under the sea in your very own submarine. Either way, you're sure to get a *stream* of visitors loving your new room, along with oceans of fans wanting to share your Sea Monster Munch!

Beach Basics

To create a cool-dude surfer's or beach babe's room, try starting off with a sandy Beach Floor. Oh, I do like to be beside the seaside!

BEACH FLOOR
💎 78 Rox

Off the Wall

Either add to your relaxed *beach-mosphere* with the simple Blue Wallpaper or dive a bit deeper into your Rox and purchase the Wavy Borders Wallpaper to totally go with the flow.

BLUE WALLPAPER
💎 17 Rox

SURFBOARD DOOR
💎 53 Rox

Surf

Surf's up, dude, and it's time to get with the surfer spirit! Casually cruise to the DIY store for a totally bodacious Surfboard Door. You'll be superstoked with the result!

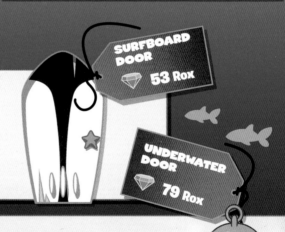

UNDERWATER DOOR
💎 79 Rox

Unda da Sea!

Alternatively, you could try the ultimate in underwater dreamworlds with the Underwater Door and the Sea Floor. It's just like the beach but wetter. Shipwrecks, sea monsters, urchins, and more—don't you love the sea? Have it all with the Underwater Wallpaper. Buy yourself a Diver's Fishtank. But you might want to watch your fingers with this surprising tank!

SHARK CABINET
💎 90 Rox

TENTACLE CHAIR
💎 62 Rox

MOS 7221

Fishy Furniture

There should definitely be something fishy going on in your room, so a Shark Cabinet is a must. Just make sure your items don't fall into its mouth! You'll find it hard not to get sucked into buying a Tentacle Chair—and you'll also find it hard to stand up when the suckers get you!

SUBMARINE WINDOW
💎 44 Rox

SEAWEED WINDOW
💎 49 Rox

Way-Out Windows

You need to get the Seaweed Window—it's like the sea came in and left you a present. Alternatively, get a Submarine Window and imagine you're, like, totally under the sea!

RED BEACH TOWEL
💎 70 Rox

SHARK BOWL
💎 103 Rox

Rad Aqua Accessories

It's ... like ... totally obvious, that you'll, like, need some Beach Towels, dude, so pop over to Yukea and decide on green, blue, or red. Now you can, like, pretend to be on the beach without all that sand in your fur!

Feel like you're missing some aquatic action? Get a Shark Bowl from Bizarre Bazaar—it's more interesting than your usual fishbowl.

COLOR CRAZY

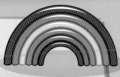

So, you like one color and nothing else? Not a problem—Monstro City has it all ready and waiting for you . . .

Mellow Yellow

If you're feeling bright and sunny, yellow may be the color for you. Try the Citrus Yellow Wallpaper for that *tangtastic* lemon look or Sunny Wallpaper for a happy mood. Then "bottom" it all off with a lovely Yellow Jelly Floor—wobble and bounce your way to the other side.

SUNNY WALLPAPER
💎 20 Rox

YELLOW JELLY FLOOR
💎 141 Rox

GREEN SLIME WALLPAPER
💎 27 Rox

GREEN DOOR
💎 27 Rox

Clean Green

A green room is sure to make those green-eyed monsters green with envy! Try the Green Cabinet and Green Slime Wallpaper, then grab a Green Door from the DIY store. And if you've really got a thing for green, buy the Dark Green Wallpaper, 'cause you can't get any greener than that, can you?

Think Pink

If you're feeling rosy, overload on pinkness with either the Yummy Pink Wallpaper from Yukea or the Pink Geometry Wallpaper. Create a total pink palace with a Pink Door or a Rounded Pink Door, plus a Curvy Pink Window. Once your pink creation is perfected, prance around in your Pink Feather Boa, Pink Tutu, and Pretty in Pink Sneakers. Pink perfection!

PINK GEOMETRY WALLPAPER
💎 67 Rox

ROUNDED PINK DOOR
💎 14 Rox

HEART WINDOW
💎 162 Rox

HEART-SHAPED BEANBAG 86 Rox

PURPLE DOOR 44 Rox

PURPLE PUZZLE SHELF 39 Rox

Purpleluscious

If your favorite color is purple and you can't resist sitting in purple comfort, you have to get the Purple Chair or the Heart-Shaped Beanbag. Then grab a Purple Door and a Purple Puzzle Shelf and transform everything into your purple dreams with a Purple Table—it makes clear drinks look purple. Purple-tastic!

BLUE STRIPES WALLPAPER 55 Rox

CURVY BLUE WINDOW 24 Rox

BLUE DUNGAREES 42 Rox

True Blue

If you're calm and collected, try the Blue Stripes or hypnotic Blue Swirls Wallpaper to keep you cool. Or escape with the beautiful Sky Wallpaper and a Blue Window. Then dress down in your Blue Dungarees, chill out, and listen to some music . . . "Blue room, I saw you standing alone!"

Tyra's Hip Tip

Monstro City is a pretty colorful place, so there are lots and lots of colors to choose from. Keep an eye out for the ones that catch your eye. Or, if you just can't decide, try going for lots of colors at the same time with the Rainbow Stand, Rainbow Chair, and Rainbow Painting—multicolored madness! Love it!

CANDY SWEET

If you have a sweet tooth and indulgent taste (and taste buds!), then this is the room for you. Grab a Gingerbread Monster (tastes better than a real monster) and curl up on your Marshmallow Pillow for plenty of sweet dreams!

Delicious Decor

There's a luscious licorice assortment of sweet wallpapers to choose from in Monstro City. Try the Cotton Candy Wallpaper. It's made with 100 percent less sugar than normal cotton candy. Or perhaps the Yummy Pink or Dark Pink Wallpaper will delight your taste buds? Sweetest of all is the Gingerbread Wallpaper—just be careful your monster doesn't eat all the way through!

DARK PINK WALLPAPER
💎 **20** Rox

YUMMY PINK WALLPAPER
💎 **41** Rox

GINGERBREAD WALLPAPER
💎 **108** Rox

Candy Crazy

If you feel so inclined, you can fill up on a whole room of candy! Buy a Candy Window—a hole in the wall with a whole load of candy. Then add the Candy Cane Door—a sweet candy cane door with a chocolatey center. Keep all your sweet clothes neat with the Candy Coathangers and stick your clothes to the Candy Standy. Then buy a Lollipop Lady—it's a doll that you can eat. YUM!

CANDY WINDOW
💎 **89** Rox

CANDY CANE DOOR
💎 **97** Rox

Sweet Little Extras

Chomp! It's time to stick your mouth together with the Gumball Machine. Goody gumdrops!

GUMBALL MACHINE
💎 51 Rox

Easter Selection

If it's Easter time, look out for the Easter Bunny Cuddly Human, Easter Bunny Ears, and Basket of Easter Eggs on sale near you. You can give eggs to all your friends or eat them all yourself.

BASKET OF EASTER EGGS
💎 47 Rox

BUNNY CUDDLY HUMAN
💎 89 Rox

WAFFLE HOUSE FLOOR
💎 56 Rox

LIMITED EDITION: Jelly Bean Wallpaper is limited-edition wallpaper for Jelly Bean Day. Tasty!

Waffle-licious
The yummiest floor around is the Waffle House Floor—mmm, waffles!

JELLY BEAN WALLPAPER
💎 100 Rox

TOFFEE CRUNCH COUCH
💎 93 Rox

Snack Break

After all that decorating, take a sweet snack break. Relax in your Toffee Crunch Couch, and slip and slide as you sit. Then, curl up on your Marshmallow Pillow from the Cloudy Cloth Clipper. Sweet dreams, sweetheart!

MARSHMALLOW PILLOW
💎 37 Rox

AZTEC/JUNGLE

Feeling culturally cool and want to delve into history? Ever wanted to be a tribal or Amazonian warrior? Try creating your own Aztec Empire or Amazon Jungle in your room by using these ancient tips, and satisfy your cultural inklings.

Aztec Antics

Give your room a sense of history and mystery with the Aztec Door. It's a door to a hidden secret temple . . . and the outside of your house. Then grab an Aztec Window, so you can go all tribal with these window borders. Now's the time to look the part. Start with the Shield— for your protection and the whole of the Monstro Kingdom!

AZTEC DOOR
◆ **80** Rox

AZTEC WINDOW
◆ **42** Rox

AMAZON WARRIOR SHIELD
◆ **153** Rox

Warrior Wardrobe: Rule the jungle with the awesome Amazon Jungle Warrior Armor, Tiara, Sandals, Shield, and Sword, which is as sharp as a sharp thing and ready to swing with you through the jungle! Me monster warrior, you nothing! *Ahhh, ahh, ahh, ahh, ahh!*

AMAZON WARRIOR ARMOR
◆ **99** Rox

AMAZON SANDALS
◆ **52** Rox

AMAZON SWORD
◆ **68** Rox

Pyramid Room

Go perfectly pyramid at Babs' Boutique with Pyro's Pyramid Floor (get the sand in your toes!), Pyro's Pyramid Wallpaper (wise mysterious hieroglyphs), Pyro's Pyramid Windows, and Pyro's Pyramid Door. Top off the sense of ancient mystery with an Egyptian Cat Statue and some Tribal Masks. Now walk like an Egyptian round and round your room!

PYRAMID WINDOW
73 Rox

PYRAMID DOOR
184 Rox

EGYPTIAN CAT STATUE
190 Rox

JUNGLE TEMPLE DOOR
200 Rox

JUNGLE TEMPLE WINDOW
185 Rox

JUNGLE TEMPLE WALLPAPER
435 Rox

Amazon Jungle-listic!

Be a *jungleist* at the DIY store and get the Jungle Temple Door—step inside and see what ancient jungle mysteries you can uncover. Then add a Jungle Temple Window—these ancient monuments let you see through to Monstro City. Mysterious! Treat your room to the ancient jungle feel with Jungle Temple Wallpaper. And finally, be careful not to let the vines wrap around your monster's feet with your Jungle Temple Hut!

HOLIDAY HAPPINESS

All monsters loooove the holidays! And it's always a great excuse to go shopping for new stuff! Whether it's Twistmas, Halloween, Valentine's Day, or Talk Like a Pirate Day, why not decorate to celebrate? Most of these items are only available during the holidays, so pick them up when you can!

TWISTMAS

It's the most monstrous time of the year! Add a festive feel to your home by buying Twistmas Presents and Crackers. When you get them home, they burst to reveal the gorgeous surprise gifts inside! Now, sit back and wait for Santa to arrive . . .

TWISTMAS PRESENT
◆ 10-110 Rox

TWISTMAS CRACKER
◆ 20-120 Rox

HALLOWEEN

Trick or treat? Even if the Haunted House theme isn't for you, it's fun to get a little creepy at Halloween! Why not try collecting this gruesome group of Jack-o'-Lanterns to cast a gloomy glow over your room?

JACK-O'-LANTERN
◆ 55 Rox

JOKE-O'-LANTERN
◆ 60 Rox

JUNK-O'-LANTERN
◆ 50 Rox

VALENTINE'S DAY

Roses are red, violets are blue, monsters are freaky, and so are you! Show your monster how much you care with these lovely Valentine's treats for their romantic room.

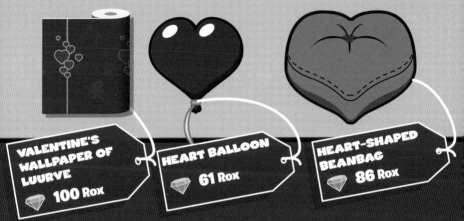

VALENTINE'S WALLPAPER OF LUURVE
💎 **100** Rox

HEART BALLOON
💎 **61** Rox

HEART-SHAPED BEANBAG
💎 **86** Rox

TALK LIKE A PIRATE DAY

Cap'n Buck's favorite holiday be Talk Like a Pirate Day! Thar be lots o' *booty-rific* items for pirate monsters! Aaaaarrrrrr!

💎 **107** Rox

💎 **212** Rox

💎 **50** Rox

CHAOS THEORY

Going through a bit of an identity crisis? Bored with the same old themes? Why not mix and monster-mash it up! The best of the rest of the rooms are the Garage Room, Doodle Room, Cloud Room, Circus Room, Star Dressing Room, Stage Room, and Snow Room, and you can even mix them all together with some of these irresistible items. Go on, go chaotically crazyyyy!

MONSTER MAKEOVER!

Before you commit to making any purchases, why not try out
some ideas on the room below using your stickers?

AND THERE'S MORE!

So now you've got your room all decorated—good job! But did you know the fun doesn't have to stop there? If you're a member and you save up your Rox, you can pop down to New Houses on Ooh La Lane and extend your home by buying new rooms! AND you can even change the style of the outside of your house—how exciting is that?

The classic starter home for every monster moving to Monstro City. But what's that hiding in the bushes?

Moshi Style
 400 Rox

Love the hustle and bustle of the big City? The Skyscraper pad oozes glamour amongst the grime!

Skyscraper Style
 1000 Rox

Haunted House Style
 1100 Rox

Ooooh, scary! What's that lurking in the attic? There's something funny about that tree, too . . .

Yummy, yummy. Check out this edible treat of a house! Perfect for monsters who are candy crazy!

Cakehouse Style
 2000 Rox

My favorite! Your little pink Poppet will feel right at home in this pretty Princess Castle. One of the turrets even makes a beautiful sparkly rainbow appear when you click on it!

Princess Castle Style

 1600 Rox

Tree House Style

1400 Rox

The Tree House is perfect for the monster that wants to get back to nature! Check out the cool tire swing and try clicking on the basket to deliver goodies to the upper levels!

Mountain House Style

1700 Rox

Get away from the hustle and bustle of Monstro City and move out to the High and Mighty Mountains in this charming hideaway.

Tyra's Hip Tip

If you're adding an item to your house, make sure you're in the room you want to keep it in before taking it out of your chest.

COOL COLLECTIBLES

There are soooo many cool and crazy collectibles in the stores around Monstro City, it's hard to know where to start. I've put together some helpful checklists for some of my faves so you can keep track of your collections and find out where to look out for them!

DESIGNER DUCKS

These little quackers are only available from Cap'n Buck's Cloudy Cloth Clipper when he's been on a trip to Bubblebath Bay!

Rubber Duck
Let it swim across your floor all day long!
💎 **18 Rox**

Toxic Duck
Green. But not in a good way.
💎 **19 Rox**

Moo Duck
Is it a duck? Is it a cow? Who cares, I want one!
💎 **20 Rox**

Roar Duck
Tiger stripes! On a duck! Two key trends in one!
💎 **23 Rox**

Inksplot Duck
What do you see in the inksplot?
💎 **21 Rox**

Pinky Duck
Pink for Poppets.
💎 **22 Rox**

CUDDLY HUMANS

Ah, look at their little human faces!
Go on, give them a hug!

Cuddly Human
Look, it's a tiny businessman!
 23 Rox

Cuddly Fisherman
Reel in the Cuddly Fisherman today!
 77 Rox

Easter Bunny Cuddly Human
With bunny ears! Double cute!
 89 Rox

Cuddly Plumber
Plug any leak with your Cuddly Plumber! (But don't blame me when he gets soggy.)
 81 Rox

Cuddly Vampire
Cuddly Coffin not included!
 92 Rox

Cuddly Ninja
Loves a stealthy hug!
63 Rox

Cuddly Pirate
Give him a cuddle, arrrr!
50 Rox

Cuddly Cowboy
Be careful he doesn't lasso your monster!
 66 Rox

Tyra's Hip Tip

If you have a Furi, dress him to impress and match your Cuddly Human with this tip-top bowler hat!

Bowler Hat
 84 Rox

BOWLER BALLS

These superstylish balls are available in a range of great colors to complement any theme! The best part? They're lickable! Taste each flavor! Pop down to the Bizarre Bazaar to bag a ball!

Yellow Bowler Ball 38 Rox

Purple Bowler Ball 36 Rox

Green Bowler Ball 50 Rox

Orange Bowler Ball 33 Rox

Blue Bowler Ball 36 Rox

TOTEM TROLLS

These mystic monsters are superstackable, so head down to Horrods and pile 'em high!

Orn
75 Rox

Ug
100 Rox

Ngue
125 Rox

Aer
150 Rox

Igg
175 Rox

SCARE BEARS

These cuddly critters make a great addition to any room, but many of them are only available at Babs' Boutique, so they're a members-only luxury!

Scare Bear
The classic Scare Bear to start your collection with. Available at the Bizarre Bazaar.
29 Rox

Patch
Stitched together from eighteen other bears!
59 Rox

Candy
Cute little Candy loves pink, so she would look perfect in your princess-themed room!
79 Rox

Spike
The bear that rocks!
99 Rox

Chip
Too cool for school.
89 Rox

Daisy
The hippie bear that likes to keep things green (even though she's blue).
109 Rox

Goldie
Put your sweatbands on and pump it with Goldie!
69 Rox

Cupcake
She smells as sweet as she looks!
95 Rox

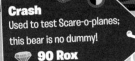

Crash
Used to test Scare-o-planes; this bear is no dummy!
90 Rox

Milk
Udderly adorable for that farm-fresh feel!
100 Rox

BEANIE BLOBS

Another members-only craze, these teenie brilliant Beanies are only available at Babs' Boutique. A bouncing bargain at only 88 Rox each!

ONLY 88 Rox each

Grin-E

Baba

Huri

Caspar

Abra Cazebra

Dimple

Arry

Ernie

Red Wolf

Inci

Bonkers

Flash

Jiffy

MYSTERY EGGS

With two series of mystery eggs to collect so far, keep an eye out for more of these delights next time you pop into Horrods.

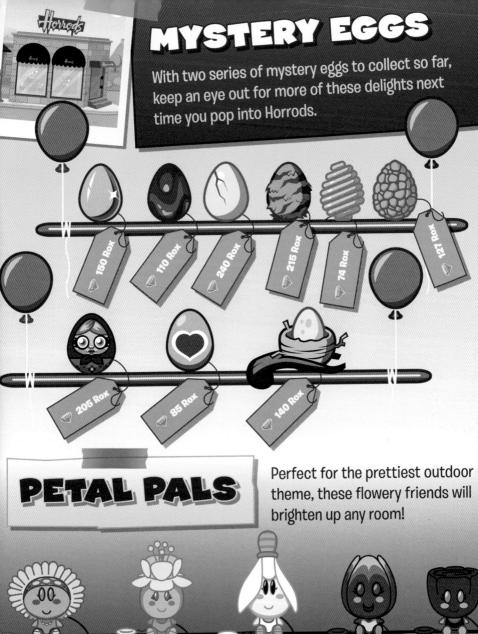

150 Rox

110 Rox

240 Rox

215 Rox

74 Rox

127 Rox

205 Rox

85 Rox

140 Rox

PETAL PALS

Perfect for the prettiest outdoor theme, these flowery friends will brighten up any room!

Dandy
166 Rox

Buttercup
156 Rox

Snowdrop
143 Rox

Tulip
190 Rox

Rose
177 Rox

WALLSCRAWL LETTERS

BABS' BOUTIQUE

Spell out your monster's name or a message to friends with these colorful letters! Available from Babs' Boutique to members only!

10 Rox **A**

30 Rox **B**

30 Rox **C**

20 Rox **D**

10 Rox **E**

40 Rox **F**

20 Rox **G**

20 Rox **H**

10 Rox **I**

80 Rox **J**

50 Rox **K**

10 Rox **L**

30 Rox **M**

10 Rox **N**

10 Rox **O**

30 Rox **P**

100 Rox **Q**

10 Rox **R**

10 Rox **S**

10 Rox **T**

10 Rox **U**

40 Rox **V**

40 Rox **W**

80 Rox **X**

40 Rox **Y**

100 Rox **Z**

BUBBLE-BLOWIN' PUZZLE

Once you hit levels 22 and up, you can collect the nine pieces of this picture puzzle from the DIY shop and pin them to your wall for a funny monster scene! Only 125 Rox each!

ONLY
125 Rox each

ARCADE GAMES

If you really want to have the best room in Monstro City, you're going to need to start saving those Rox! You need at least 500 to buy one of these arcade games from the Games Starcade on Sludge Street, but they're well worth the investment!

BUG'S BIG BOUNCE

Bounce your way to the top of Monstro City and beyond! How far can you make Bug bounce? Hint—black clouds will disappear when you jump on them, but rainbows will give you a bouncing boost!

Bug's Big Bounce
💎 **500 Rox**

OCTO'S ECO ADVENTURE

Keep Monstro City clean! Shoot the trash before it gets in the water and score big! Hint—shooting falling stars helps Octo fire farther!

Octo's Eco Adventure
💎 **700 Rox**

SEA MONSTER MUNCH

Chomp your way through as many fish as possible, but be careful not to hit your own tail! Hint—the more you eat, the bigger you'll grow!

Sea Monster
Munch
850 Rox

Grab your stunt bike and collect as many stars as you can in this high-speed downhill dash! Hint—cycle up the ramps to reach the higher stars!

Downhill Dash

950 Rox

MOSHLINGS!

No home is complete without a pet, and Moshlings are little pets for your monster! Any monster can keep up to two Moshlings in his or her room, but Moshi Members can collect many more! Moshi Members can have up to six Moshlings roaming around their house and can keep the others in their Zoo. Here's how to find a furry (or sticky or even ghostly) little friend for your monster.

HOW DOES YOUR GARDEN GROW?

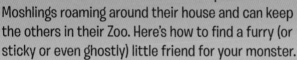

By now you've probably discovered that your little house has a garden! Buy some seeds from the Seed Cart on Main Street or Super Seeds at the Port and pick a combination of three kinds to plant in your garden. The flowers might take some time to grow, but remember, a happy monster's flowers grow the fastest!

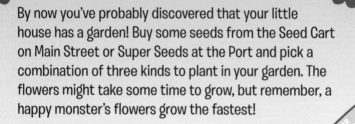

CLUEKOO!

Once all three flowers have grown, there's a chance you might have attracted a Moshling to your garden. If not, the Cluekoo will give you hints on how to find one. Sometimes you'll need to grow the flowers in a certain color, so you might have to keep trying to get the one you need.

MY MOSHLING?

If a Moshling has showed up, you can choose whether to keep it or set it free. Keeping the Moshling will send it into your home, while setting it free will let it continue to roam wild!

If you attract a Squidge or a DJ Quack and you already have one, you can still keep it if you want, and build up a flock!

THE ZOO

The number on your Zoo's door tells you and your friends how many kinds of Moshlings you have collected so far. Inside your Zoo, you can see all the Moshlings in their pens. When you have all four Moshlings from a set, cool themed wallpaper will appear behind them!

Decide which Moshlings you want to have in your room by clicking on the IN YOUR ROOM sign and the Moshlings in their pens to swap them in and out.

Tyra's Hip Tip

Here's a sneaky seed code for you to try! If you get the colors right, this attracts one of my absolute favorite Moshlings—she fits in perfectly with any Egyptian theme!

ROX, ROX, ROX!

Of course, this awesome stuff doesn't come for free! You're going to need lots of Rox to do all this shopping! Here are some of the best ways to earn your Rox in Monstro City...

PUZZLE PALACE

Push the Puzzles button in your room to be taken to Puzzle Palace! The Daily Challenge is the best way ever to earn lots of Rox, but you can only do it once every twenty-four hours, so don't forget to test yourself every day!

The Hall of Puzzles has lots more smaller tests that you can play as many times as you like, and each one is worth 5 Rox.

RECOMMEND A FRIEND

Check out the link on screen underneath your room—if you recommend a friend and they sign up to Moshi Monsters, you get a whopping 150 Rox! They'll even get a massive Friendship Trophy to add to their rooms!

 INVITE FRIENDS. GET ROX!

Whoever told you money doesn't grow on trees was lying! Moshi Members can pop to the Port and shake Rox down from the trees!

SHAKE IT, BABY!

FLUTTERBY FIELD

Help Colonel Catcher save the Flutterbies from a bug invasion and win Rox! Rare Flutterbies are worth more, so catch them quick!

EN-GEN

Join the Roarkers and help generate Monstrowatts for Monstro City by rotating blox and connecting four or more of the same color!

ICE-SCREAM!

There's always a job going at the Ice-Scream parlor! Earn your Rox by keeping up with the customers' orders. But don't forget to pick up your tips!

THE UNDERGROUND DISCO

Dance your way to success at the Underground Disco! The higher your score from Simon Growl, Roary Scrawl, and yours truly, the higher your Rox prize will be!

GROW YOUR OWN

Sometimes, when you plant seeds in your garden, a Rox plant will grow instead of a flower! Dig it up to claim your Rox!

HOT SILLY PEPPERS
MOON ORCHID
STAR BLOSSOM
SNAP APPLE
LOVE BERRIES
DRAGON FRUIT

MONSTAR ROOMS!

Don't forget to take a look around Monstro City and visit other monsters' rooms for inspiration. You don't have to become friends with them first, just click on any monster in the street and you can go and see what they've done with their place!

Use these pages to take notes on your favorite rooms and the things they have that you'd like to look out for! Stick a star on the ones you think deserve to be MonSTAR rooms!

Monster Owner	Monster Name	⭐ Inspirations ⭐	Room Rating

Monster Owner	Monster Name	⭐ Inspirations ⭐	Room Rating

TYRA'S FINAL THOUGHTS

That's a wrap! A little insight into my world as a home-fashion expert and all the amazing things I've seen on my tours! I hope you picked up some useful ideas, but don't forget, Monstro City is changing and growing all the time. There's always something new to buy, a new theme to try, a new place to shop at, or a new way of earning Rox—a monster's home is never finished, you know!

DON'T FORGET . . .

 1. Buy it when you see it! Sometimes, that great little accessory that caught your eye might not be there the next day, so try to pick things up when you see them.

 2. There's always something awesome you can do with your room, whatever level your monster is at—but the higher your level, the more fun things become available for you to buy. So keep playing to open up new treasures!

 3. Lucky Moshi Members get access to special stores and things to buy down at the Port!

 4. Keep checking out other monsters' rooms and always rate what you see! It's nice to give feedback and let them know when you think their room rocks.

 5. Always be ready! Keep an eye on the *Daily Growl* for my next home-fashion tour and make sure your room is at its best. Next time, the MonSTAR of the show could be you!

Check out these other great Moshi Monsters books!